cloverleaf books™

Alike and Different

My Clothes, Your Clothes

by Lisa Bullard

illustrated by Renée Kurilla

M MILLBROOK PRESS · MINNEAPOLIS

For Grandma T. —L.B.

Millbrook Press
A division of Lerner Publishing Group, Inc.
241 First Avenue North
Minneapolis, MN 55401 USA

For reading levels and more information, look up this title at www.lernerbooks.com.

Main body text set in Slappy Inline 18/28.
Typeface provided by T26.

Library of Congress Cataloging-in-Publication Data

Bullard, Lisa.
    My clothes, your clothes / by Lisa Bullard ; illustrated by Renée Kurilla.
        pages cm. — (Cloverleaf Books™ — Alike and Different)
    Includes index.
    ISBN 978-1-4677-4902-2 (lib. bdg. : alk. paper) —
ISBN 978-1-4677-6030-0 (pbk.) — ISBN 978-1-4677-6291-5 (EB pdf)
    1. Clothing and dress—Juvenile literature. I. Title.
GT518.B85 2015
391—dc23   2014025257

Manufactured in the United States of America
1 – BP – 12/31/14

TABLE OF CONTENTS

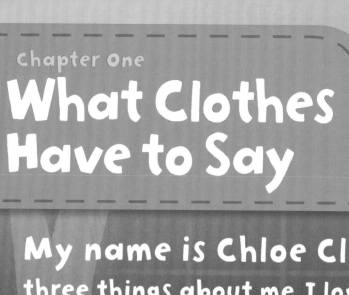

Chapter One

What Clothes Have to Say

My name is Chloe Clark-Li. Here are three things about me. I love my new karate class. I'm going to be a firefighter when I grow up. And my school uniform makes my elbows itch!

4

That's why I'm so excited about Friday. It's a special dress-up day at my school. **No uniforms!** Mama says I can pick out my own outfit. But I'm not sure how to choose!

Mama reminds me that clothes do more than just cover us. "Clothes help tell the world things about us," she says. Uh-oh! What if my clothes blab all my secrets?

Clothes do say something about people! Mama wears her uniform to work. But my other mom wears business suits. Their work clothes show one way they're different.

I ask my cousin Jordan what his clothes say about him. He points to his jersey. "This tells people **I like football**," he says. "And it lets other fans know if we cheer for the same team."

Is there something you wear that shows you're part of a group or a team?

I guess clothes can also show how people are alike! Mom says that's why we wear school uniforms too. It helps everybody feel they belong at our school.

Chapter Two
Clothes and Community

Mama, Mom, and I pick up my sister, Lexi, at high school. Lexi is happy that she doesn't have to wear a uniform. **She likes to wear clothes that look really different from everyone else's!** Today she's wearing her Chinese dress. Mom's family came from China.

I tell Lexi that Mama said people speak through their clothes. "She's right," says Lexi. "Look over there. **Can you guess which boy wants to be a country music star?**"

At home, I ask Mama how else clothes speak for someone. She shows me pictures of Amish people. Mama explains **the Amish wear very plain clothing for religious reasons.**

She says they want to look different from the world around them. But within their own community, **Amish people don't want to stand out.**

My friend Katie usually wears the same kind of clothes I do. But she has one dress that even sounds special. **When she dances at powwows, she wears her jingle dress.**

Katie says jingle dresses are part of her family's traditions. Ojibwe women and girls wear them to **celebrate their culture.**

My neighbor Ben has a little cap called a **kippah** that is part of his family's culture. He wears it at his Jewish synagogue.

And my friend Sadia wears a head covering when she leaves her house. She tells me **her special scarf is called a hijab.** She says some Muslim women and girls wear it for religious reasons.

Do you ever wear clothes from a special community or culture?

Chapter Three

Changing Clothes

I don't wear anything on my head for my religion. But I do dress up to go to church on Sundays. Mom says it's a way of showing respect. **And I like being fancy sometimes.**

Afterward, it's fun to go home and put on my comfiest clothes. **I especially love my bunny slippers!** I wear them so often that Mama says we better buy more carrots.

People wear different kinds of clothes to do different things. What kind of clothes do you most like to wear?

Chapter Four

The Big Decision

It's time to choose my outfit for our dress-up day at school. **There's so much to think about!** I remember where my family comes from. I think about what I like now and who I want to become. Finally, I've decided!

What do you think? Will my choices tell the world who I am?

Make a Paper Bag Vest

You can make your own dress-up clothes for a costume or playtime. Here's an easy way to make a vest out of a paper bag!

Supplies needed

scissors
paper grocery bag

markers, stickers, aluminum foil, glue, construction paper, glitter glue, or other things to decorate your vest

Directions

Ask a grown-up to help you cut the bag. Cut the lines as shown in the pictures.

1) Cut a line all the way up the middle of the bag, running from the bag opening to the center of the bottom panel.

2) Cut a hole large enough for your head out of the center of the bottom panel.

3) Cut armholes on each side of the bag, about 2 inches (5 centimeters) from the bottom of the bag.

4) If the bag has writing on it, turn it inside out. The bottom of the bag is now the top of your vest (where your head goes).

5) If you want to, cut fringe along the bottom of the vest.

6) Decorate your vest!

GLOSSARY

Amish: a conservative Christian group that lives simply, dresses plainly, and focuses on their families and community

hijab: a head covering worn by some Muslim women

Jewish: related to the religion called Judaism or to the people known as Jews

jingle dress: a dress worn at American Indian powwows that is decorated with rows of metal cones that jingle when the wearer dances

kippah: a small cap traditionally worn by Jewish men and boys but today also worn by some women and girls

Muslim: a follower of the religion of Islam

Ojibwe: a North American plains Indian people

powwows: gatherings of American Indians who come to celebrate, pray, and socialize

religious: belonging to a system of faith and worship

synagogue: the place where Jewish people meet for worship

BOOKS

Ajmera, Maya, Elise Hofer Derstine, and Cynthia Pon. *What We Wear: Dressing Up around the World.* Watertown, MA: Charlesbridge, 2012.
See children from all around the world dressed in clothes ranging from those for every day to those for special events.

Ashburn, Boni. *I Had a Favorite Dress.* New York: Abrams, 2011.
Find out how one girl wears her favorite dress in different ways as she grows older.

Seiss, Ellie. *Olivia and the Fashion Show.* New York: Simon Spotlight, 2011.
Olivia decides to design her own clothes when those at the fashion show turn out to be boring.

WEBSITES

Children's University of Manchester
http://www.childrensuniversity.manchester.ac.uk/interactives/art&design/talkingtextiles/costume/
Play a matching game to learn more about clothes from around the world.

Girls Go Games: Fashion Designer New York
http://www.girlsgogames.com/game/fashion-designer-2.html
Play fashion designer by putting together outfits for fashion models.

LERNER SOURCE™
Expand learning beyond the printed book. Download free, complementary educational resources for this book from our website, www.lernersource.com.

7